Hodder Toddler

This book belongs to:

....

D1343571

For Lukas and Ernie
x x x

SQUEAK! SQUEAK!
by Siobhan Dodds

British Library Cataloguing in Publication Data
A catalogue record of this book is available from the British Library.

ISBN 0 340 79943 9 (PB)

Copyright © Siobhan Dodds 2001

The right of Siobhan Dodds to be identified as the author and illustrator
of this Work has been asserted by her in accordance with
the Copyright, Designs and Patents Act 1988.

First edition published 2001
10 9 8 7 6 5 4 3 2 1

Published by Hodder Children's Books
a division of Hodder Headline Limited
338 Euston Road London NW1 3BH

Printed in Hong Kong

Squeak! Squeak!

by Siobhan Dodds

Hodder
Children's
Books

A division of Hodder Headline Limited

Nelly is wearing her new shoes.
'Look, Grandad! I can march!'

'Knees up! Knees down!'
sings Grandad, as they march out
into the kitchen.

All of a sudden, there's a squeak!

Squeak!

'That sounds like the squeak, squeak of a squeaky toy,' says Grandad.

They look under the table but there is no toy to be found.

'Look, Grandma, I can twiz and twirl!'

'Round and round,' laughs Grandma,
as they twiz and twirl down the hall.

All of a sudden, there's a squeak!

Squeak!

'That sounds like the squeaky wheels of a tricycle,' whispers Grandma.

They look out of the window but there is no tricycle to be seen.

'Look, Mummy, I can make
big monster steps!'

'Thump! Thump!' shouts Mummy,
as they make big monster steps
into the bedroom.

All of a sudden, there's a squeak!

Squeak!

'That sounds like the squeak, squeak of a mouse,' whispers Mummy.

They look on top of the wardrobe but there is no mouse to be found.

'Look, Daddy! I can bunny hop!'
'Bouncy! Bouncy!' laughs Daddy,
as they bunny hop into the playroom.

All of a sudden, there's a squeak!

Squeak!

'That sounds like the squeak, squeak
of the hamster on its wheel,'
says Daddy.

They look in the cage
but the hamster is asleep.

Just as Nelly jumps down there's
another squeak!

Squeak!

'I know what it is!'
laughs everyone together.

'It's the SQUEAK, SQUEAK
of Nelly's new squeaky shoes!'

Goodbye
Hodder Toddler